ON THE ROAD!

written by Claire Philip

Illustrated by Mike Moran

MILES
KELLY

Busy roads

Every day, people use different vehicles to travel on the roads.

Pick-up truck

This is a motorway, a road where vehicles can drive faster than on normal roads.

Super car

Ambulance

Always wear your seatbelt!

Sharing a car is fun too!

Tow truck

Saloon car

Vroooom!

Most cars give out harmful gases, so sharing a car is better for the planet.

Motorbike

Off to school

Lots of children travel to school by bus! This is an American school bus.

The bus stops at different places to pick the children up.

If you live close enough to your school you might cycle, walk or even ride a skateboard or scooter.

Travelling together

Double-decker sightseeing buses take tourists to see famous landmarks around a city.

I have an open top with no roof!

City bendy buses have a special section called a bellow that allows them to turn around tight corners.

Bellow

I'm much longer than other city buses!

Low-floor buses have no steps onto the passenger cabin – this makes it much easier for everyone to get onboard.

I also have a ramp that slides out.

Coaches take people on longer journeys. They are more comfortable than buses.

Coaches have toilets, TVs – even wireless Internet!

Luggage hold

All kinds of cars

When you're out and about, you'll see many different types of cars.

Classic car

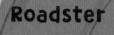

Roadster

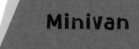

Minivan

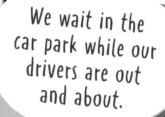

We wait in the car park while our drivers are out and about.

Micro car

Estate

Convertible

Great! A parking space!

Going electric

Vehicles that run on electricity are better for the environment (and us!) because they do not give out nasty fumes.

Charging point

Electric car

My car has a rechargeable battery!

The battery is plugged into an electric point to charge, just like a plug in a house!

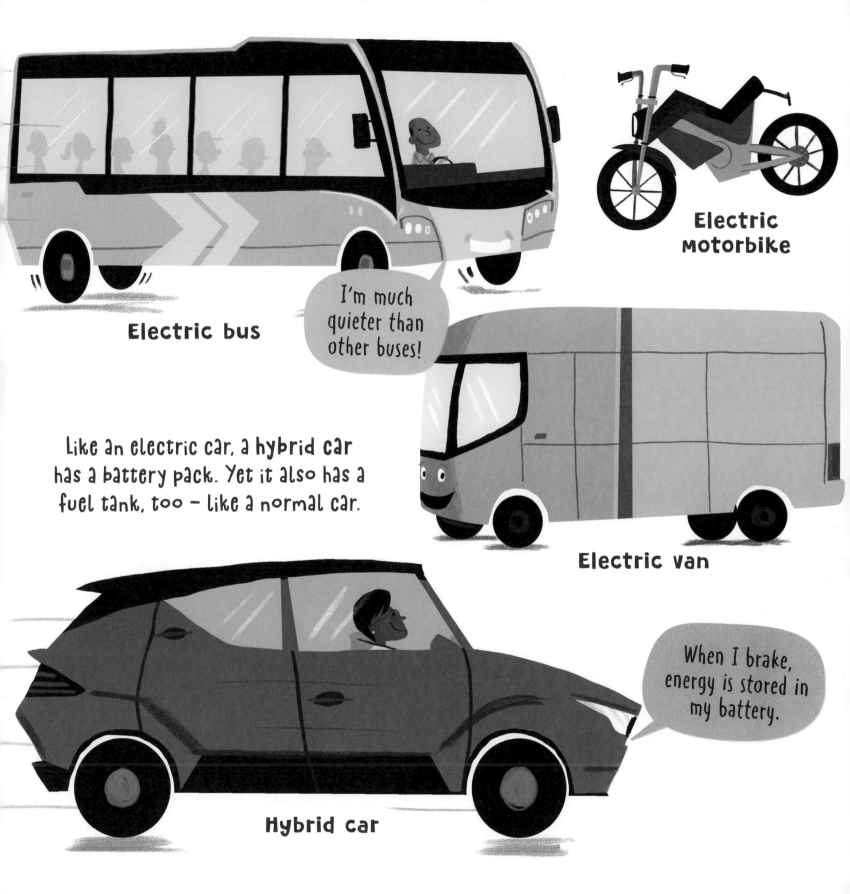

Electric motorbike

Electric bus

I'm much quieter than other buses!

Like an electric car, a hybrid car has a battery pack. Yet it also has a fuel tank, too – like a normal car.

Electric van

When I brake, energy is stored in my battery.

Hybrid car

On two wheels

A person powers a bicycle by pushing the pedals.

Pedal

Mountain bike

Road bike

Most bicycles and motorbikes have two wheels set in a frame.

Touring motorbike

Hybrid bike

I'm a mix between a road bike and a mountain bike.

Recumbent cycle

Tandem

Roooar!

A motorbike has an engine.

Road superbike

Moped

Sport bike

Cruiser

Scooter

Chopper

Motorbike and sidecar

Help at hand

Cars, trucks and motorbikes help emergency workers race to the rescue.

Ambulances carry medical equipment to treat people that are ill or injured.

Police motorbikes are very useful for weaving through heavy traffic.

Flashing lights make us easy to see!

Fire engines carry special equipment to put out fires and rescue people or animals!

Police cars have noisy sirens to warn people that they are coming through!

Busy city!

Meet some of the vehicles that people use to get around busy city roads.

People in cities often use rideshares, cars that they hire using their smartphones.

Beep! Beep!

Many cities have bikes that people can hire.

Taxi

TAXI

Rideshare car

Public-use bike

Scooter

Tuk-tuk van

cool trucks

Trucks are large vehicles that can carry super heavy loads. They come in all shapes and sizes.

Articulated truck

Fuel tanker

Painted truck

In Pakistan, trucks often have amazing decorations!

Double-trailer lorry

Ice cream van

Dekotora truck

I'm from Japan! My decorations are so bright and colourful!

Dumper truck

Honk!

Logging truck

Car transporter

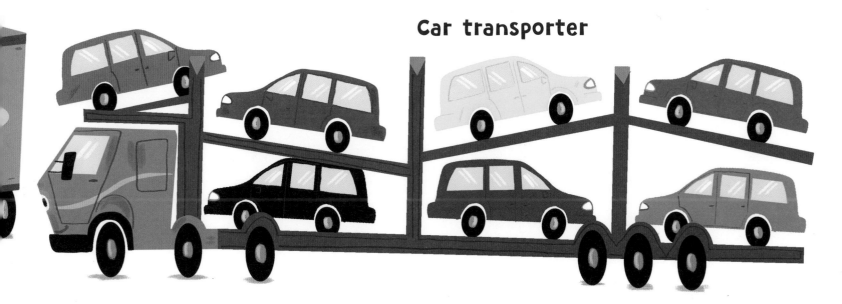

Holiday time!

Some vehicles can be used as holiday homes.

You can cook, sleep and shower inside a motorhome!

We're staying at a campsite.

Touring caravans are towed behind another vehicle. They can be small and simple or more luxurious.

I have a kitchen, bathroom and bedrooms inside!

Tow bar

Time to work!

Have you seen any of these busy working machines in action?

Road sweeper

Concrete mixer

Spreading salt on the roads stops them from getting icy in freezing weather.

Gritting lorry

I have a mechanical arm, which lifts the bins and tips the rubbish in.

Off the road

These vehicles are known for being extra fun to drive!

Go-cart

Jeep

I'm ready to race!

Race car

I speed over sand dunes.

Quad bike

I can do amazing jumps and flips!

Monster truck